Christmas Shorts

by Matt Hoverman

A SAMUEL FRENCH ACTING EDITION

SAMUEL FRENCH

FOUNDED 1830

NEW YORK HOLLYWOOD LONDON TORONTO

SAMUELFRENCH.COM

4|12
8⁹⁹

•

ISBN 978-0-573-69894-1   Printed in U.S.A.   #29697

MUSIC USE NOTE

Licensees are solely responsible for obtaining formal written permission from copyright owners to use copyrighted music in the performance of this play and are strongly cautioned to do so. If no such permission is obtained by the licensee, then the licensee must use only original music that the licensee owns and controls. Licensees are solely responsible and liable for all music clearances and shall indemnify the copyright owners of the play and their licensing agent, Samuel French, Inc., against any costs, expenses, losses and liabilities arising from the use of music by licensees.

IMPORTANT BILLING AND CREDIT
REQUIREMENTS

All producers of *CHRISTMAS SHORTS must* give credit to the Author of the Play in all programs distributed in connection with performances of the Play, and in all instances in which the title of the Play appears for the purposes of advertising, publicizing or otherwise exploiting the Play and/ or a production. The name of the Author *must* appear on a separate line on which no other name appears, immediately following the title and *must* appear in size of type not less than fifty percent of the size of the title type.

CHRISTMAS SHORTS was first produced as an "Angels in Progress" Workshop by Naked Angels (Geoffrey Nauffts, artistic director) at the Main Stage Theatre in New York City in December 2008. The performance was directed by Suzanne Agins. The cast was as follows:

Stephanie Brooke

Marylouise Burke

Craig Carlisle

Paul DeBoy

Christina Kirk

Chris Stack

THE STUDENT was one of the winners of the 2009 Samuel French Off Off Broadway Short Play Festival, 34th series. It was directed by Suzanne Agins, and featured:

HUGH . . . . Craig Carlisle
BURT . . . . Steven Hauck

CHARACTERS

There are multiple ways to cast these plays. I suggest:

ACTOR A - (an "Archie", perhaps tall and fair, goofy - with the ability to adopt a patrician air): **BURT** in *The Student*, **SAM** in *The Christmas Witch*, **NED** in *Xmas Cards*, **BOB** in *Nativity*

ACTOR B - (a "Reggie", could be dark and a little heavy, master of the slow burn): **GREG** in *Going Home*, **HUGH** in *The Student*, **JOE** in *The Christmas Witch*, **JIM** in *Nativity*

ACTRESS A - (a "Betty", maybe blonde, open-hearted and dotty): **CHERYL** in *Going Home*, **NELLY** in *Xmas Cards*, **JULIET** in *Nativity*

ACTRESS B - (a "Veronica", probably brunette, a barracuda who can also be vulnerable): **KAREN** in *The Christmas Witch*, **JOAN** in *Nativity*

All actors are in their 30s – early 40s (although sometimes they play older, as indicated). If there are funds for two additional actors, an older actress could play **NELLY** in *Xmas Cards*, and an older actor could play **BURT** in *The Student* and **NED** in *Xmas Cards*.

A NOTE ON TONE

One day in acting graduate school, a well-known actress was brought in to explain to us how casting directors categorize actors according to their "most essential quality." The categories included: Sex, Intelligence, Danger/Violence, Humor, Beauty, etc. Qualities like "sex" and "beauty," she elaborated, refer more to your inner energy than your outside physique. As we went around the room, guessing our types, I reflected on my big heart, and when it was my turn, I declared, "Beauty! I think I'm beauty!" There was a pause, and then everyone fell out of their chairs, laughing. She said, "Honey, you're humor."

Although this experience sent me straight to therapy, it also captures the tone of my plays. Actors who tend to succeed in my work are really funny, but also really real. If you play my stuff like a sketch, it'll fall flat. But if you go for the beauty – if you find the heart in each character, in each play (and every one has one) – you'll get the laughs. And hopefully you'll move the audience too.

For Terry Dion, my 3rd grade teacher,
who told me I could write a play...

GOING HOME

(A couch, a table, a tiny Christmas tree on the table, with a single strand of unlit lights. There is an iPod and a small speaker unit on the table too. GREG sits on the couch, talking to CHERYL, off. [They're both just 30.])

GREG. Hey Cheryl, I just downloaded some great new albums off iTunes. Do you want to listen to *Jessica Simpson: Hanukkah Hottie* or *A Very Metallica Christmas?**

CHERYL. *(off)* They both sound so good.

GREG. I also got a recording of "The Night Before Christmas" read by Ol' Dirty Bastard and Yo-Yo Ma.

CHERYL. *(off)* Maybe put it on shuffle.

GREG. Good idea.

CHERYL. *(off)* Greg, can you do earphones, honey? I'm trying to concentrate in here.

GREG. Yeah, all right.

(He puts in earbuds, hits play.)

GREG. *(singing à la Jessica Simpson, with seated dance moves.)*
"I have a little Dreidel
I made it out of clay
And when it's dry and ready
Dreidel I will play...*baby!*"

(He takes out one earbud.)

GREG. Oh my god, this is hilarious, you have to hear this. What are you *doing* in there?

CHERYL. I'm on the computer.

GREG. *(sighs)* Okay.

(He hits a button, plays air guitar, and sings in a menacing Metallica vein.)

---

* See 'Two Last Notes' on page 52.

GREG. *(cont.)*

"Oh, you better watch out

You better not cry

You better not pout

I'm tellin' you why

Saaanta Claus is comin' to town...*while you sleep!*"

(He stops the music.)

This is no fun without you. Come on in here.

CHERYL. *(off)* I'm on the phone!

GREG. Who you calling?

CHERYL. *(off)* I'm on hold.

GREG. *(grumbling)* Okay. That didn't really answer my question, but...

(Beat. He pulls a small box out of a bag. He opens the box and pulls out a single ornament.)

Hey Cheryl, wait'll you see the tree I got at the deli. It's huge! I think it's going to take all day to hang our ornament. Cheryl?

(no answer)

Seriously Cheryl, this is going to be the best Christmas ever. No taking the train to my mother's house, or taking the bus to my father's ice fishing shack. No waiting in line at the airport to fly to your parents'. No crazy uncles or aunts or sister or brothers or nieces or nephews, no fistfights, or medical emergencies, or calls to 911, no trips to jail to bail out your half-brother. Oh my god, no jello molds! Free at last, free at last, thank god almighty we are free at last! Yes, we can! Hey Cheryl, I'm proud of you for resisting the urge to go home this Christmas, you know? It shows real growth. Don't worry, we're going to have a blast! I know the plan was ice skating in Central Park, but what if, we just went to like, three movies tomorrow, in a row instead? How's that grab you?

*(Enter **CHERYL**, in a winter coat, with luggage. She is dead serious.)*

(beat)

GREG. *(cont.)* What's in the luggage, Cheryl, ice skates?

CHERYL. I'm sorry, Greg. I can't do it.

GREG. What?

CHERYL. I can't do it. I can't abandon my family. I'm going home.

GREG. Aw, no.

CHERYL. I hope you'll understand.

GREG. But it's too late. It's already Christmas Eve!

CHERYL. No. If I leave right now, I can make it by dawn tomorrow, just in time to get my presents beneath their tree.

GREG. But we sent them presents, Cheryl. We sent them a box of presents a month ago, remember?

CHERYL. Not stocking stuffers.

GREG. Where are you gonna find stocking stuffers now?

CHERYL. *(holds up a stuffed tube sock)* I put a bunch of your toiletries in your tube socks. My dad needs shaving supplies.

GREG. So do I! You stole my stuff?

CHERYL. You can get your own. You're very resourceful. You don't need me like they do.

GREG. I can't believe this.

CHERYL. I've called a cab.

GREG. You're going to take a cab to Wisconsin?

CHERYL. Greg, they have these things called airplanes.

GREG. You have a ticket? How long have you been planning this?

CHERYL. About seven minutes. I went online. I got a last minute fare.

GREG. That must have cost a fortune.

CHERYL. It's worth it. I love my family, Greg.

GREG. Cheryl, your family is the Addams family.

CHERYL. Greg, don't start. I need you to just let me go with kindness.

GREG. Cheryl, you know it's true. Your parents' place is the Hotel California. You can check out anytime you like, but you can never leave.

CHERYL. You're being very ungracious. My parents like *you.*

GREG. Your parents don't even like each other! They tell the same five stories every time we get together. It's like Dessert of the Damned over there.

CHERYL. Their marriage is what it is.

GREG. Your father sired a child with another woman!

CHERYL. David and his wife Ling Ling are part of our family now. I love them.

GREG. David and your brother Paul get into a shouting match every Christmas! Last year David broke Paul's nose.

CHERYL. That's why I need to be there. To protect my baby sister.

GREG. Trish is 27 years old. She can fend for herself.

CHERYL. She still lives at home, Greg.

GREG. That is my point. You have to get out, Cheryl. You have to get out or *you're* going to be spending your days knitting the dog sweaters.

CHERYL. Trish has a *talent.*

GREG. Oh my god, you've totally lost it.

CHERYL. Well, I can't expect you to understand this, Greg. You don't like your parents.

GREG. I like my parents.

CHERYL. You like them to be far away from you.

GREG. With good reason. The last time I saw my dad, he shot at me.

CHERYL. He was drunk.

GREG. Yeah, exactly, he was drunk with a loaded shotgun.

CHERYL. He didn't have his glasses on. He thought you were your mother. He loves you, Greg. And if you spent more time with him, you'd see that.

(beat)

GREG. You've been watching the Hallmark Channel, haven't you?

CHERYL. *(lying)* No.

GREG. You've been watching Christmas specials again, haven't you?

CHERYL. No. I mean, I may have seen a holiday commercial or two...

GREG. You know you're susceptible to advertising at this time of year, Cheryl.

CHERYL. That polar bear cub befriended that Eskimo hunter with just a bottle of Coca Cola, Greg. Think what we could do if we approach our parents with the same spirit of forgiveness and peace!

GREG. Do you remember last Christmas? After we came back, you went into a depression for four days.

CHERYL. That's because you've turned me on them. You made me get depressed. I was happy with my family. But you've kidnapped me emotionally. Anything I may have said to the contrary can be attributed to the Stockholm Syndrome.

GREG. I've *kidnapped* you?

CHERYL. Yes. Because you hate families. You hate all families. You're a family hater.

GREG. You're a family hater too, Cheryl, for 362 days out of the year. But every Christmas, Thanksgiving and Easter you develop selective amnesia and like a salmon swimming upstream to its birthing place, you writhe across the country back into the womb of that Midwestern Gothic horror show, and for what?

CHERYL. To see my mommy and my papa!

GREG. You're thirty years old, woman! You're a successful events planner for a big corporation! You have health insurance and a 401K! You're married!

CHERYL. We always go caroling at our neighbors!

GREG. Your neighbors call the cops on you. When it's two a.m., it isn't caroling, it's trespassing!

CHERYL. My mother always makes her special vegetable soup!

GREG. It's just table scraps in a pot of boiling water. I swear, last year, she threw in dog food!

CHERYL. We have an ice cream birthday cake for Jesus!

GREG. We can have our own rituals, Cheryl. We can have our own traditions.

CHERYL. No! No, I can't listen to you. You are the devil. Family-hater!

GREG. Please stop calling me that!

CHERYL. You need to know what you are!

GREG. I love families, Cheryl! I love our family! You and me! *We're* a family.

CHERYL. We're not a family. We're a couple.

GREG. A couple's a family. We're a family.

CHERYL. Not in my book.

GREG. What book is that?

CHERYL. The book of "Get out of my way, Greg." The book of "If I don't get to the airport by nine, I'll miss my flight and it's the last plane available!"

(**CHERYL** *tries to push past* **GREG.**)

Let me go! Let me go, Greg!

GREG. No, I won't!

CHERYL. Rape! Rape! Christmas is being raped!

(**GREG** *tackles* **CHERYL** *on the couch.*)

GET OFF OF ME!

GREG. Do you remember what happened last year, Cheryl? Remember how after your brother got his nose broken, and the neighbors called the cops, and your mother passed out in the sweet potatoes, and your father tried to hook up with Ling Ling...do you remember how we got laid over in O'Hare, and we spent New Year's Eve on a cot by the luggage carousel? Do you remember that?

CHERYL. *(dizzy)* ...Vaguely.

GREG. Do you remember what you said to me as we lay there in rows with all the other miserable holiday travelers?

CHERYL. No...

GREG. You said, "Please Greg, no matter what I say. Do NOT let me go home for Christmas next year." I don't hate your family. I love *you.* I want to spend Christmas with my wife. We don't have to be satellites anymore, Cheryl. We don't need to orbit around anyone else. We can be the center of our own galaxy. We can have our own gravitational pull. Look, I got us a tree. Our first tree.

(As he turns to show her, **CHERYL** *knees him in the balls and gets away.)*

Oof!

CHERYL. I'm sorry, Greg. It's just this one last time. If I'm not there, I'm afraid they'll all just – die.

(Beat. **CHERYL** *stops at the door.)*

GREG. What's wrong?

CHERYL. I can't go.

GREG. Why not?

CHERYL. I don't know. My feet won't move. They're stuck to the floor. I can't go.

(Beat. He slowly rises and goes to her.)

GREG. Maybe it's gravity.

CHERYL. Greg, I've never not gone home for a holiday.

GREG. I know.

CHERYL. I had strep throat in college, when I was doing my semester abroad in Paris, and I still came home for Mothers' Day.

GREG. I know.

CHERYL. *(tearing up)* What are they going to do without me?

GREG. The same thing they always do.

CHERYL. What am I going to do without them?

(beat)

GREG. Thrive.

(beat)

CHERYL. I feel so empty. I feel like I don't exist.

GREG. You do exist.

CHERYL. I'm not part of anything.

GREG. You are. You're part of me. You're part of this.

CHERYL. What is *this?* It's just a fifth floor walk-up in the East Village.

(They are back on the couch. He places the ornament in her hands.)

GREG. Look, I bought it today. It's our first ornament. Hang it on our tree.

(CHERYL looks at the tree.)

CHERYL. It's so – small.

GREG. It'll grow. In time, it'll grow.

(She slowly, painfully, hangs the ornament on the tree. He claps his hands twice, the lights go out, except for the Christmas tree lights.)

Is this so bad?

CHERYL. No.

(She relaxes into his arms.)

GREG. Want to listen to some music?

CHERYL. Yes.

(He presses a button on the iPod.)

CHERYL. Next year, can we get a dog?

GREG. Next year, I'm chaining you to the radiator.

CHERYL. *(smiles)* It'll be our holiday tradition.

(Cello holiday music. And then a gruff rapper's voice says:)[*]

VOICE OF OL' DIRTY BASTARD. *(V.O.)* 'Twas the Night Before Christmas
And all through the place
Not a creature was stirring
'Cept this *bitch on my face...* "

(CHERYL giggles.)

(blackout)

End of Play

THE STUDENT

*(A classroom. **HUGH** [30s-40s, heavy], a writing teacher in a corduroy jacket, talks on his cellphone. It's a high school classroom, so his desk is adult-sized, but the student's desk/chair combo is a little small.)*

HUGH. *(on phone)* Hey honey, just one more student conference and then I'm home. What's with the tone? Oh my god. A letter came for me today from *Harper's*, didn't it? I knew it. What does it say, I know you opened it. No, you don't have to read it. I know it by heart. "Thank you very much for giving us the opportunity to read 'Beer Goggles' and for your patience in hearing from us. We receive thousands of submissions a year and do our best to read them all. Unfortunately, we do not have a space for 'Beer Goggles' at this time." And then there's a hand-scrawled note at the bottom that says, "Keep submitting, Hugh!" NO NOTE? Okay, Merry Christmas! Fuck *Harper's*. Fuck them. I'm fine. I'll see you later. Right after I destroy this one last student. Bye.

*(In a foul mood, **HUGH** goes to the door, opens it and speaks off.)*

Enter at your own peril.

*(**HUGH** sits. Enter **BURT**, a businessman [50ish], in a suit, carrying a business shoulder bag. He's very uptight and has a reverence for his teacher.)*

BURT. Hello, Mr. Simms. Merry Christmas.

HUGH. Yeah yeah. Fuck Christmas.

BURT. *(sits in the small chair/desk combo, hurriedly pulling out a notebook)* Is this a writing exercise?

HUGH. What?

BURT. I'm referring to your unorthodox teaching style. Do you want me to do a ten minute free write on the theme of "Fuck Christmas"?

HUGH. No, no. *(considers it)* Actually – *(decides against it)* No. Don't do that. Let's just talk. I'm sorry, Burt. I'm in kind of a foul mood today.

BURT. Use it.

HUGH. What?

BURT. That's what you tell us to do, right, Mr. Simms? Start with how we're feeling in this moment. Don't deny the body. The body tells you what to write.

HUGH. Yeah, just between us, that's bullshit, Burt.

BURT. I don't think so.

HUGH. It is, Burt. It's bullshit.

BURT. You're just testing me or something.

HUGH. No. No, I'm not. I'm leveling with you for the first time all semester. I don't know what the fuck I'm talking about. I'm a hack. And no one wants to read my writing. And you were foolish to sign up for a class taught by someone who doesn't know what the fuck he's talking about.

(beat)

BURT. Do you want me to write for ten minutes about that?

HUGH. No, Burt, no. I want you to see the truth about me. I'm a failure. I know nothing. I have nothing to impart. Nothing to give you. I have no wisdom, no technique, no skill. Any advice I give will probably destroy your story and ruin any chance you have of ever seeing it published anywhere. I'm an anti-teacher, do you see that? I am not a mentor. I am a *de-mentor.* I will destroy the budding artist within you.

(short beat)

So, let's go over your story, shall we?

BURT. Um, okay.

HUGH. *(paging through a manila folder)* Now let's see, which rough diamond belongs to *Burt?*

BURT. Mine's called "Simon the Gay Elf."

HUGH. *(still looking)* "Simon the Gay Elf"...

BURT. I don't want to be published.

HUGH. What?

BURT. I didn't sign up for this class to write a story to get it published.

HUGH. You didn't? Why not?

BURT. I came to this class because I wanted to learn how to tell a story. My story. Well, I mean, first I came because I got laid off and my employment coach suggested it would be a good way to work on my storytelling skills. She said, when interviewing for a new position it's important to be able to frame your experience as a compelling, empowering narrative. So that's why I signed up. But then I got you as a teacher and my – priorities changed.

HUGH. What do you mean?

BURT. Well, you told us to write what was in our heart.

HUGH. And – ?

BURT. And, so I wrote what was in my heart.

HUGH. *(finding Burt's story)* "Simon the Gay Elf."

BURT. Yes.

HUGH. You wrote about a gay elf.

BURT. Yes.

HUGH. One of Santa's little helpers is queer.

BURT. Yes, that's the premise.

HUGH. Aren't they all gay?

BURT. No, you'd think so, but apparently it's quite a stigma.

HUGH. You've done research?

BURT. In my imagination.

HUGH. Are you gay, Burt?

BURT. Absolutely not. Why do you ask?

HUGH. You said you wrote what's in your heart.

BURT. I'm happily married. But I have a – a feeling for men who like other men. Especially very, very small men who like other men.

HUGH. I think they call that pederasty.

BURT. No, not children –

HUGH. You like midgets.

BURT. No.

HUGH. Dwarves.

BURT. No.

HUGH. "Little people."

BURT. No, elves. I like elves. I like magical, helpful, pointy-shoed homosexual elves.

HUGH. Okay. Let's deal with this piece structurally.

(*tiny beat*)

Does your wife know you like gay elves?

BURT. I showed her the story.

HUGH. What did she think of it?

BURT. She didn't like it very much.

HUGH. No, I'll bet not.

BURT. She's sort of angry at you, actually.

HUGH. Me, why?

BURT. I told her you told me to write it.

HUGH. I don't remember assigning –

BURT. You told me to open a vein in my arm and stick the pen in it and let the river of my spirit flow out onto the paper.

HUGH. That does sound like me.

BURT. You're my favorite teacher. Ever.

HUGH. Okay. Okay, let's talk about this story. I'm actually kind of glad to hear you say you're not aiming at publication, because I was confused by the intended audience. At first, it seemed like I was reading a fairy tale for kids, but then it got pretty graphic.

BURT. What part was graphic?

HUGH. The part about Simon's gigantic penis.

BURT. That's actually real.

HUGH. More imaginative research?

BURT. No, I looked it up. A human dwarf can have shrunken arms and legs and other organs that are regular sized. And because the rest of their body is so small –

HUGH. It makes the penis seem gigantic by comparison.

BURT. That's what I read.

HUGH. So you're just trying to educate the kids.

BURT. No, this isn't for young audiences.

HUGH. I didn't think so, no.

(**HUGH** *takes a moment to read a passage of the story to himself.* **BURT** *looks at him admiringly.*)

BURT. *Your* hands are small.

HUGH. Hm?

BURT. *(changing the subject)* What did you think of my portrayal of Santa?

HUGH. Well, he wasn't very jolly!

BURT. No, he wasn't.

HUGH. He seemed kind of conflicted.

BURT. Yes, he is.

HUGH. *(reading)* I – thought it was interesting that Simon chose Santa Claus, to lust after someone so inaccessible.

BURT. Yes, that is the tragedy of Simon the Gay Elf. He can never express his longing.

HUGH. One of the notes I had was that I wasn't sure why Simon was so obsessed with Santa Claus. I mean, why wasn't he going after Gunther the burly elf who worked the bellows in the blacksmith shop, or Hercule the glass blowing elf? These seem like much better matches for Simon. Why does he fall for a fat old married guy?

BURT. Because his love is impossible, Mr. Simms. It will undo his whole life, the whole fabric of the elf code. He had to bury his desires so long ago. It's only when he gets fired from his job as an accountant at the candy cane processing plant that he has the time to think about his life and the direction it's taken. It's only then that he is open to chance, and to the happy accident of running into Santa in the reindeer stables. Of course he would fall for Santa. Santa is the giver of gifts, the believer of possibility, the maker of magic. Santa is the one who lets him ride on Rudolph and when he asks, "But how will I know where to steer him?", Santa replies, "Just follow your heart." How could he not love him? With everything he has inside of his little elf body – with the big gigantic penis?

HUGH. Burt, do you know I'm married?

BURT. Yes, to Mrs. Claus.

HUGH. Do you know I'm straight?

BURT. Yes, and so am I.

HUGH. But I'm *really* straight.

BURT. I won't hold that against you.

HUGH. Burt, –

BURT. I wrote this story for you, Mr. Simms. I wrote this story for you. I think you're brilliant.

(*Beat.* **HUGH** *takes in the compliment.*)

HUGH. Thank you.

BURT. Do you see the story?

HUGH. Yes.

BURT. Do you see me?

HUGH. Yes, I do, Burt. Thank you. It's a beautiful story.

BURT. And it's sad too, isn't it?

HUGH. Yes, it is.

BURT. But it's true. It's real.

HUGH. Yes, Burt, it's real.

BURT. You believe in Simon the gay elf?

HUGH. Yes, I do. I'll never forget him.

BURT. Thank you, Mr. Simms. Merry Christmas.

(**BURT** *hands him a wrapped box and rises to go.*)

HUGH. Burt, call me Hugh.

BURT. I'd rather not. I need the distance.

(Exit **BURT.***)*

*(***HUGH** *dials his cellphone.)*

HUGH. *(on phone)* Hi. I'm sorry about before. I was just disappointed. I'll be home in a few. Do you need anything?

*(***HUGH** *opens the box, there's a Santa Claus hat inside it. He looks at it for a moment.)*

Oh, you know student conferences. They're a little tiring. But they're important.

(He puts on the Santa hat.)

When you're a teacher.

(blackout)

End of Play

(Note: I suggest you make **BURT**'s *gift box a narrow, rectangular box, so that the audience suspects the gift inside is phallic. The Santa Claus hat can be rolled up inside it, so when* **HUGH** *pulls it out of the box, it unfurls for a nice comic reveal.)*

THE CHRISTMAS WITCH

(An apartment. Two dudes in their mid-30s. On a couch in front of a TV, or on two La-Z-Boys. They have blankets on their laps and plates of food.)

SAM. Remote control?

JOE. Check!

SAM. Spiked eggnog?

JOE. Check!

SAM. Microwaved turkey grinders from the 7-Eleven?

JOE. Check!

SAM. No ladyfriends?

JOE. Double check!

SAM. *(toasts his roomie)* Merry Christmas, Joe.

JOE. *(toasts back)* Merry Christmas, Sam.

SAM. To us – two dudes, livin' the dream!

JOE. To us!

(They drink.)

SAM. *(gags a little)* What did you spike this with?

JOE. Budweiser.

SAM. Good choice. So guess what I got you.

(holds up a wrapped gift that is clearly a DVD case)

JOE. Ultimate Fighter, Season 3?*

SAM. No.

JOE. Ultimate Fighter, Season 4?

SAM. No.

JOE. Ultimate Fighter, Season –

SAM. Joe, it's not Ultimate Fighter.

---

*See 'Two Last Notes' on page 52.

JOE. What is it, Sam?

SAM. SANTA VS. DRACULA.

JOE. No.

SAM. Yes.

JOE. No!

SAM. Yes!

JOE. But that's not even out yet!

SAM. Poppa's got a connection!

JOE. Holy Nosferatu Noel! Did you see the trailer online?

SAM. I emailed you the link!

JOE. I know but did you watch it?

SAM. We watched it together, Joe!

JOE. I know but do you remember what happened?

SAM. What, when they showed the house at night?

JOE. And it's all quiet?

SAM. And the children are tucked in their beds?

JOE. And Santa's sleigh lands on the roof?

SAM. And Dracula and his minions fly out of the chimney like bats?

JOE. And they put Santa in a headlock!

SAM. And they make him watch them eat the reindeer!

JOE. And they drizzle the reindeer blood on Santa's white white beard.

SAM. And Dracula whispers in his ear, "Now evil rules the night, fat man."

JOE. And Santa looks up at him with his rosy cheeks –

SAM. And his ruddy nose –

JOE. And his bloody beard –

SAM. And he says, "But it isn't night, vampire scum, it's day!"

BOTH. And there's fucking Rudolph behind them, coming out of the sky –

SAM. With his nose on fire!

JOE. His nose is a meteor!

SAM. His nose is the motherfucking SUN!

JOE. And although it drains every last bit of energy in his reindeer body, Rudolph fries all those vampires where they stand with his beams of reindeer light!

SAM. Rudolph sacrifices himself for the friend he loves!

JOE. With his friendship laser beams of death!

SAM. And all that's left of the Prince of Darkness is a single stocking.

JOE. Smoking in the moonlight.

SAM. Like a tiny chimney.

JOE. Or a smoking stocking.

SAM. Yeah.

JOE. Yeah.

    (beat)

SAM. Yeah, they really show a lot in trailers today.

JOE. Yeah, I can't imagine what else would be in the movie.

SAM. Let's bag it.

JOE. Sounds good. Besides, Karen's coming over.

SAM. What?

JOE. Karen's coming over.

SAM. No. No!

JOE. Oh, come on, I told you that.

SAM. No, you didn't. When?

JOE. When you were in the shower.

SAM. Dude, that is so not cool.

JOE. Sam. Sam...

SAM. No, man, this was *our* night. Now it's going to be horrible. This happens every Christmas!

JOE. Dude, you've got to stop being afraid of Karen.

SAM. Afraid? She terrifies me!

JOE. She's not that bad.

SAM. She's evil, Joe. She is the spawn of Satan. She makes me pee my pants.

JOE. One time!

SAM. *(rises, panicked)* When is she coming? I have to be in my room when she gets here. I can't let her see me. I freeze in her stare.

JOE. Why do you react like this every year?

SAM. The woman isn't right, Joe. She laughs at crippled children.

JOE. That's just a nervous laugh. She gets nervous around people with disabilities.

SAM. She laughs at the homeless!

JOE. That's just a nervous tic.

SAM. She cheated on you on your birthday!

JOE. One birthday, Sam. And it was with Marcos.

SAM. She told you it was your fault!

JOE. Well, it was, kind of. I wasn't satisfying her in bed.

SAM. And why not?

JOE. Because I wasn't Marcos.

SAM. She's a witch, Joe. Karen is the Christmas Witch.

JOE. There's no such thing as the Christmas Witch.

SAM. An evil old girlfriend who gets lonely every holiday season and calls you up because she doesn't want to face the desperate hollowness of her shallow life on Christmas eve? You bet there is a Christmas Witch, compadre.

JOE. I don't know. I think she's changed.

SAM. She hasn't changed.

JOE. She said she feels remorse.

SAM. The Christmas Witch feels no remorse.

JOE. She apologized to me.

SAM. When?

JOE. Yesterday. On my Facebook fun-wall.

SAM. What did she apologize for?

JOE. For what she said when she broke my heart.

SAM. And what was that, Joe?

JOE. I don't want to get into –

SAM. What did she say, Joe?

JOE. Just that we should break up. Because I was holding her back sexually, intellectually, artistically, financially and politically.

SAM. She's going to crush you.

JOE. I can see her tonight without getting sucked in, Sam. I'm stronger this year.

SAM. You're a *snack* to her. She's in your head. Are you having the dream again?

JOE. I don't remember my dreams.

SAM. Are you having *the dream?*

JOE. The one where she murders my family and cuts them into pieces and puts them into bloody garbage bags?

SAM. Yes.

JOE. And says, "I killed them because I love you."

SAM. Yes.

JOE. Maybe once or twice. But it's a *wet* dream!

SAM. I can't let you do this, Joe. You deserve so much better.

JOE. How do I deserve better, Sam? I'm 35 and I'm still living with my college roommate.

(beat)

SAM. (wounded) That is a point of pride, Joe.

JOE. You're right, I'm sorry.

SAM. You really hurt me just now, Joe.

JOE. I'm sorry, Sam, but sometimes I wonder if what you and I have is enough to sustain me forever.

SAM. Joe, you know as well as I do that there is no greater love than that which exists between two dudes living the dream.

JOE. ...I know.

SAM. I love you, dude.

JOE. I love you, dude.

SAM. You see what she does? She makes you doubt your values!

JOE. God, she makes me feel so bad about myself!

SAM. That's what I'm saying!

JOE. She makes me want to just kill myself!

SAM. Yes! So what are you going to do about this?

>   *(beat)*

>   *(The doorbell rings.)*

JOE. Take her out to dinner?

SAM. No! You're going to send this evil away, Joe. Back into the hole in the ground from which it crawled. It's Jesus' birthday.

JOE. *(In a tiny voice, as he is drawn inexorably to the door.)* …I can't.

>   *(JOE opens the door. Enter KAREN.)*

JOE. Hey there.

KAREN. Hi, you.

JOE. It's Joe.

KAREN. I know.

>   *(a tentative, awkward kiss)*

JOE. You look nice.

KAREN. Change your shirt.

JOE. I'll be back in a minute.

>   *(JOE exits. SAM starts to follow.)*

KAREN. Where you going, Sam?

>   *(uncomfortable beat between KAREN and SAM)*

SAM. *(rigid with fear)* Hey there.

KAREN. How're things?

SAM. Great. Working hard. Lately I've been volunteering. With paraplegic kids.

KAREN. *(giggles)* Oh really? That sounds rewarding.

SAM. Yeah, they're mostly all homeless.

KAREN. *(more giggles)* Wow. Touching.

>   *(Then KAREN laughs for a long time.)*

SAM. So how's Marcos?

KAREN. Marcos and I – didn't work out.

SAM. What did you – do to him?

KAREN. What could I do? He was holding me back – sexually, intellectually, artistically, financially and politically.

SAM. That sounds familiar.

KAREN. I've been doing a lot of soul searching, Sam, and a very small amount of therapy, and I've come to see that Joe is the one I want. Forever.

SAM. Oh no.

KAREN. Oh yes. I've decided to overlook his faults and allow him to try to make me feel what you call happiness.

SAM. Oh please, Christmas Witch, spare my friend! He deserves a chance at life!

KAREN. What?

SAM. Please pass him by. He's been a good boy.

KAREN. I don't know what you're talking about.

SAM. *(on his knees)* MERCY! MERCY, CHRISTMAS WITCH! TAKE ME! IF YOU MUST TAKE SOMEONE TO-NIGHT, TAKE ME!

KAREN. Why would I take you?

SAM. I don't know! Because...you haven't tasted my flesh yet? Because I haven't had sex in so long it's like my virginity grew back? Because I'm willing to sacrifice myself because I love my friend?

*(**KAREN** gets real close to **SAM**. She kisses him, hard, with tongue. He makes himself return the passion, with difficulty.)*

KAREN. *(close to **SAM**)* Do you like that?

SAM. *(terrified, but with courage)* ...Yes.

KAREN. Do you want more of that?

SAM. *(ditto)* ...Uh huh.

KAREN. Do I smell urine?

SAM. ...A little bit, yeah.

KAREN. All right, it's a deal. I'll take you. Let's go.

SAM. Let me just leave Joe a note.

KAREN. No note. I hunger *now.*

> *(As **KAREN** pulls **SAM** out, he quickly takes off a shoe and sock and leaves the sock behind in the middle of the floor.)*
>
> *(beat)*
>
> *(Enter **JOE**, in a new shirt.)*

JOE. Sorry that took so long, but I seem to have lost all confidence in my ability to even dress myself.

> *(Notices they're gone.)*

Karen? Sam? Guys, what happened?

> *(He finds **SAM**'s sock on the floor and picks it up.)*
>
> *(in horror)* The Christmas Witch!
>
> *(blackout)*

End of Play

XMAS CARDS

(A prosperous, conservative husband and wife in their late 50's sit in two arm chairs, about to fill out Christmas Cards. She does needlepoint. [Probably the seat cushion for a dining room chair.] He writes.)

NED. All right, Nelly, put on the Bing Crosby album and set the kitchen timer. I've got about two hours of Christmas spirit in me, and there are two hundred Christmas cards to sign. That gives me 35 seconds per card. Then I'm off to the club for an argument.

NELLY. You can do it, honey.

NED. You are my witness. I am not going to get *bogged down* in this, this year.

NELLY. You won't, Ned.

NED. Just in and out, real quick.

NELLY. That's the attitude, dear.

NED. This year, I won't fret over every little word.

NELLY. Good.

NED. I bought very small cards, so anything I write will look pithy.

NELLY. Nice touch.

NED. And I have finally accepted that I don't need to be clever.

NELLY. Well, you're *not* clever, Ned, are you?

NED. No, I'm not. Every time I try to be clever, things go awry.

NELLY. Well, you don't really like other people, and it comes through.

NED. I'm a boor.

NELLY. You are a boor. But you're my boor, darling.

NED. Thank you for your support, Nelly. I couldn't do this without you.

NELLY. I will never leave your side, Ned.

NED. *(sadly)* Yes, Nelly. I know.

(beat)

Okay, first name on the list. Bill Charles.

NELLY. Oh, I like Bill.

NED. So do I, for a Lutheran. This should be easy.

(writing)

"Dear Bill and Chloe: Happy Holidays! Ned Bingham-ton III."

NELLY. Masterful.

NED. Thank you. Letter number two –

NELLY. Are he and Chloe still together?

NED. What? Yes! I think they are.

NELLY. I thought I heard they were having difficulty.

NED. No. Are they?

NELLY. I thought I heard they were.

NED. Where did you hear that?

NELLY. *(vaguely)* I don't know, around.

NED. Oh. Well, do you think I shouldn't put her name on the card?

NELLY. I don't know. They're your letters.

NED. Well, how am I supposed to keep track of the ins and outs of other people's marriages? I'm going to leave her name in.

NELLY. *(doubtful)* Okay.

NED. You think I shouldn't?

NELLY. I just wouldn't want to offend them.

NED. Well, I don't want to offend them either.

NELLY. Of course you could offend them if they *are* together, and you *don't* put her name on it.

NED. That's true too. Maybe I should send them two separate cards.

NELLY. To the same address?

NED. I could write, "To Bill, et al."

NELLY. That's a bit formal.

NED. "To Bill and occupant"?

NELLY. What if he's living by himself in that big house on Seabrook Drive?

NED. You think she'd let him keep the property?

NELLY. I don't know, Ned. I'm not a divorce attorney.

 (Beat. **NED** *sighs.)*

NED. I'm going to set this one aside for now. Come back to it. First card and I'm already behind schedule.

NELLY. Who's the next one on your list?

NED. Fred Farmer.

NELLY. Well, you know he's single, so that's easy.

NED. That's right.

 (writing)

 "Dear Fred. Have a Happy! Best, Ned."

NELLY. Perfect.

NED. Moving on.

NELLY. How do you spell Fred?

NED. *Fred?* F.R.E.D.

NELLY. I think there's an alternate spelling.

NED. Are you insane?

NELLY. He had some property listed in the newspaper, I think his name had a silent "O".

NED. I'm not honoring a silent "O" in Fred.

NELLY. But what if it's his name?

NED. He'll survive. I'm sure I won't be the first to make that mistake.

NELLY. I'm sure he won't be hurt to realize you don't even know his *name.*

NED. Okay, so Fred with an "O".

NELLY. *(vaguely)* I'm not positive I'm right about that.

NED. Okay, we'll return to this one too. Next up: Tim Packer. I know how to spell Tim Packer! "Season's Greetings, Tim!" Done!

NELLY. Very nice. It's too short.

NED. What are you talking about?

NELLY. Well, you've known him for years.

NED. What am I expected to say?

NELLY. I don't know. It's your card.

NED. What's wrong with "Season's Greetings"?

NELLY. It's tired, Ned.

NED. He's our paper boy, Nelly. I don't have a lot to say to our paper boy.

NELLY. He's a young man. He craves father figures. Mentor him. Guide him. Set him on the right path. Like you never did for our children.

NED. In a three-by-five Christmas card?!

NELLY. Or not, Ned. I'm not a guidance counselor.

(beat)

NED. "Dear Tim. Season's Greetings. Remember, victory goes to the strong."

NELLY. It sounded different in my head.

NED. "Dear Tim. Season's Greetings. Remember, you're only twelve once."

NELLY. That's a little morbid.

NED. "Dear Tim. Season's Greetings. Never, ever get married."

NELLY. Why don't you put that one aside for now.

NED. *(does so, with resentment)* Good idea. Next one: Sarah Silvers.

NELLY. Ooo, what are you going to say to her?

NED. I'm not going to tell you.

NELLY. She's such a nice woman.

NED. *(writing, shielding it from her)* I know, and I'm going to write this all by myself.

NELLY. We haven't seen her in years.

NED. I know just the note to write to Sarah Silvers!

NELLY. She was always such a good long-distance runner.

NED. That's what I'm writing about! I remember!

NELLY. It's a shame she lost that leg in the threshing machine accident.

NED. She what?

NELLY. Severed her leg at the hip. Right before the summer Olympics. *That* was a dream denied.

(She makes the horrible grinding noise of a threshing machine accident.)

(beat)

So don't mention the running.

*(**NED** rips up the card.)*

Or was that Sarah Summers?

NED. Nelly.

NELLY. Yes?

NED. How long until you die?

NELLY. Many, many years.

NED. Then I need to say something.

NELLY. Yes?

NED. GO. AWAY.

NELLY. What?

NED. I want you to leave the house.

NELLY. But we're getting so much accomplished!

NED. You are sapping my will to live!

NELLY. But you asked me for help.

NED. I must do this alone!

NELLY. Alone? But you haven't even started on the cousins yet, and they've all had head lice this past month.

NED. *(shaking his head fervently)* No!

NELLY. You're going to need my input to address that.

NED. I'm not going to address it! I'm recklessly going to pretend I don't know it happened!

NELLY. Ned, you don't know how to write Christmas Cards.

NED. *(near tears)* No, I don't. I clearly don't. Because we're three songs into the Bing Crosby album and I haven't licked a single envelope. But a man has to draw a line in the snow somewhere. And this is mine.

NELLY. But you need me, Ned. To protect you from your own instincts.

NED. What's wrong with my instincts, Nelly? Am I so disturbed? Because I want to be brief and impersonal? Because I don't feel it's my job to assuage the soul of every paper boy and orthopedist I ever met? Am I so wrong to believe that people aren't fragile, that they could actually handle it if I wish them the wrong holiday salutation or don't remember that their kids are infested with head vermin? Am I so awful to suggest that we could treat each other like adults and not – Christmas tree ornaments! *Am I so wrong to have this dream?*

NELLY. Yes.

(beat)

Yes, you are, Ned.

(beat)

But that's what I'm here for. To show you how you do everything wrong. I'm your wife.

(He bursts into tears.)

(beat)

NED. Please, Nelly. Go. Leave me. Take the car and drive far, far away. To the Pathmark on the corner.

NELLY. Over *Christmas cards*, Ned?

NED. I'm afraid so.

NELLY. All right. All right, Ned. I'll leave you. And drive to the Pathmark on the corner. *(short beat)* I'll miss you.

NED. I'll miss you too, Nelly.

NELLY. I like writing out cards with you, Ned.

NED. But we never actually *do* write out cards, Nelly.

NELLY. But still it's something we never actually do, *together*.

(Beat. He doesn't respond. She rises to leave – brave, but hurt. She gets to the door.)

NED. Nelly, –

NELLY. Yes, Ned?

NED. I may – need some help with zip codes, in a little while.

NELLY. I could come back – in about an hour.

NED. I may have some questions about postage.

NELLY. I'll sit in the driveway.

NED. Nelly –

NELLY. Yes, my love?

NED. I could use some help with this one card. Here, I'll address it.

(He writes something inside the card and hands it to her.)

NELLY. *(She reads.)* "To Nelly Binghamton. Thank you. Love, Ned."

NED. You can fill in the rest.

NELLY. It's perfect.

(blackout)

End of Play

NATIVITY

(A man [30's] dressed as Joseph [in robes and fake beard]. A woman [30's] dressed as Mary [in robes and head scarf.] They sit a few chairs apart from each other in a medical waiting room. Mary knits.)

(Above them, a sign reads "Bethlehem, PA Fertility Clinic.")

(The woman's name is **JOAN** *and the man's name is* **BOB**. *They don't know each other. Beat.)*

BOB. Hi.

JOAN. Hi.

BOB. Whatcha knitting?

JOAN. Excuse me?

BOB. Whatcha knitting?

JOAN. I – um.

BOB. I'm sorry.

JOAN. No.

BOB. I don't mean to be rude.

JOAN. No, it's okay.

BOB. I didn't mean to disturb you.

JOAN. I don't mind. I'm just. It's a baby jumper.

(She holds it up. It's huge.)

BOB. Whoa.

JOAN. Yeah.

BOB. That's a big baby jumper.

JOAN. Yeah.

BOB. You're gonna have a big baby.

JOAN. I hope so.

BOB. I mean like Godzilla-sized.

JOAN. Do you think it's too big?

BOB. For a human baby, maybe.

JOAN. I've been working on it for a while.

BOB. Where, in a lab? Are you digging up corpses and welding them together to create some kind of Frankenstein baby?

JOAN. No, I mean I've been working on the baby jumper for a while. I've been coming here for awhile.

BOB. Oh.

(He gets it.)

Oh.

JOAN. Yeah.

BOB. You've been through this before.

JOAN. Yeah.

BOB. It didn't work out?

JOAN. Not so much, no. That's why I keep knitting. Maybe I should stop already and start on a new one, but I get superstitious.

BOB. I understand. Is that why you're wearing the costume?

JOAN. What costume?

BOB. Huh?

JOAN. Am I wearing a costume? Oh, I am! I guess I am. No, I'm kidding, I know I am. I know I am.

BOB. Okay. Ha ha.

JOAN. I'm subbing for a friend at the 11:30am St. Joseph's Christmas mass today. She had a last minute conflict. And I was the only one she could call who she knew wouldn't have any plans today. Because I'm Jewish.

BOB. Oh, okay.

JOAN. Is that weird?

BOB. No.

JOAN. Do you think that's weird? It's a little weird, isn't it?

BOB. I don't think so. I mean, Mary was Jewish, wasn't she?

JOAN. I don't really know the story.

BOB. I think she was Jewish.

JOAN. I'm kind of nervous about the whole thing. I mean, I hope I don't screw things up, or, like cause flaming stones of fire to come crashing in through the church ceiling because I'm on the stage.

BOB. Altar.

JOAN. Yeah, whatever. Same difference.

BOB. I think you'll be okay.

JOAN. I'm doing a favor for a friend. That's Christian, isn't it?

BOB. I think you'll be just fine. I'm playing Joseph in the noon nativity mass at St. Bartholomew's.

JOAN. Is that a good part?

BOB. I'm Mary's husband.

JOAN. Great. *(Tiny beat. Shyly.)* I wish you could be my husband.

BOB. What?

JOAN. No, I just, I wish you were at my church – I mean, the church I'm going to be at, then you could talk me through the whole shebang. I probably shouldn't have said yes, because this is going to take a while, and I'm going to be cutting it close. I just mean, you seem nice, that's all. I don't meet a lot of nice guys.

BOB. Thanks.

(They smile at each other.)

JOAN. I don't understand religion, you know?

BOB. I believe.

JOAN. Well, that's great, because I work in a Christian agency. I'm a social worker. And I tell you, those people go crazy about their Christmas parties. And they want to be sensitive to people like me, so they call it a Holiday party, like I care. If there's free cake, I'll be a Scientologist. But my favorite is Daralice, who's a project associate. And she's a Jehovah's Witness, – although, what did they actually witness, I've never been clear on that, you know? – and you know they don't believe in celebrating holidays, at all, like NOT

AT ALL. But these women I work with, every year they try to call the party something else to lure Daralice in. Oh, it's the Winter Solstice gathering, it's the End of Year Summation Meeting – with cake!, and every year she says, "It's a Christmas party, isn't it? Isn't it?!" "No, Daralice, no!" But she can smell out a holiday a mile away. You know what I'm saying? I just don't know what it's all about. I'm culturally Jewish, but that just means I'm a registered Democrat, it doesn't mean I *feel* anything at this time of year, or have access to any kind of – *hope.*

BOB. Where's your husband?

JOAN. He isn't here because – he – doesn't actually exist. I'm not married.

BOB. Oh. I'm Bob.

JOAN. Hi Bob, I'm Joan.

BOB. Hi Joan.

JOAN. Yeah, I'm in this alone. I mean, I've had boyfriends, don't get me wrong, some even long term. But it never seems to work out. Maybe I'm too flaky, you know, maybe they can't, just can't, finally *take* me, you know? I'm a little – I'm not for all markets. I mean, I'm delightful, in small doses. But according to Jim, the most recent one, "the fiancé," the one who left me thirteen months ago, I "attract calamity." I "draw into my life the exact opposite of what I want." He said he loved me, but he couldn't stay with me, because, well, I wanted a baby, and he had made it clear from the get go that he wasn't interested in that! Not at all! "So why was I still fighting for it?" And so, I decided to turn over a new leaf, and try to draw into my life what I actually wanted, instead of Jim, and quit waiting for a miracle and try to have a baby, whether or not I could meet a man. What do you think? You're a reasonable guy. What's your sense of me? Do you think I make bad choices? Do you think I draw to myself the wrong kind of man? The weirdos?

BOB. No.

JOAN. Thank you.

BOB. Sometimes God has a special plan for special people.

JOAN. You think so, Bob?

BOB. Yes, I do, Joan. Because I'm just like you. I'm doing this on my own too.

   (beat)

JOAN. You're what?

BOB. I'm doing this on my own too.

JOAN. Doing what?

BOB. Trying to have a baby!

JOAN. You're not married?

BOB. No.

JOAN. You have no girlfriend?

BOB. No.

JOAN. Fiancée?

BOB. Uh uh.

JOAN. Okay…

BOB. With God, all things are possible. Especially on His day. So I'm here.

JOAN. Yeah, I think you're going to be disappointed.

BOB. Why do you say that?

JOAN. You know what, Bob? Let's take a little break from talking. I need to focus on my knitting. And try to recover from coming face to face with my fate.

BOB. Where do we go to get the babies?

JOAN. You sign in at the desk right over there.

BOB. Where?

JOAN. Right there, the desk – with the sign that says "sign in here."

BOB. I'm not a strong reader.

JOAN. You're gonna make someone a great dad.

BOB. I already have all the Tinkertoys.

   (He exits towards the desk.)

JOAN. *(to herself)* Way to go, Joan. What else could happen today to make it even worse?

JIM. *(off, entering)* Joan? Joan?

(He enters with **JULIET**. *[Both in 30s.] He's a jerk.)*

JOAN. Oh my god.

JIM. Oh my god, Joan.

JOAN. Hi, Jim.

JIM. Joan, how long has it been?

JOAN. I don't know, I don't keep track.

JIM. A year?

JOAN. Thirteen months. Or so.

JIM. You look great. Are you a Muslim now?

JOAN. No, Jim. It's a costume. I'm supposed to be Mary. I'm helping out a friend.

JIM. That's great, you were always so helpful to everyone but yourself.

JOAN. And you're still such an asshole.

JIM. And *that's* why you're still alone.

JOAN. Wow. How do you know I'm still alone?

JIM. Educated guess.

JULIET. I'm Juliet.

JIM. So this is Juliet.

JULIET. Hi, I'm Juliet.

JOAN. I'm Joan.

JULIET. It's nice to meet you. Merry Christmas.

JOAN. Thanks, I'm Jewish.

JULIET. I'm sorry. I'm so nervous. I'm usually more circumspect.

JIM. Juliet, Joan's an old girlfriend.

JULIET. And now we're both here! We have so much in common!

JOAN. Yes, but I got out.

JULIET. *(confused)* Out of what?

JOAN. So, nervous, huh? What are you having done today?

JULIET. We're having an IVF procedure, fingers crossed.

JOAN. Really? That surprises me.

JULIET. I know, on Christmas day, right? But when the body decides it's the day, it's the day. It's amazing that this place is open 365 days a year.

JOAN. I know that. That's what I'm here for too. What surprises me, Jim, was I thought you didn't want to have kids?

JIM. Did I say that?

JOAN. Yes, you did.

JIM. I don't recall saying that.

JOAN. Actually, what you said, in our three years of couples counseling, while my eggs were aging, was that you loved me so much that you couldn't leave me, that I was not just your soulmate but your *soul's mate*, you wanted to make that distinction to avoid the cliché, but you just could never, ever bring yourself to be a father.

JIM. I guess something changed.

JOAN. What changed, Jim?

JIM. Who I was with.

JULIET. Jim, don't be mean, it's Christmas.

JIM. I'm not being mean. Joan is an adult. She asked me a question, and I answered it truthfully. It's important for her to hear that, because she doesn't live her life responsibly. She doesn't focus. She doesn't organize. I met someone in Juliet who can focus, who is organized, who I can trust to raise my progeny.

JULIET. I'm not that organized.

JIM. Yes, you are, Juliet, don't sell yourself short.

JULIET. I kind of left my driver's license at home, because I was nervous, and I sort of need it to sign in today.

JIM. *(to* JULIET, *aside)* Why didn't you put it in the wallet I gave you?

JULIET. I had it in the purse I was using last night when we went out to dinner.

JIM. Why do you take your licenses and cards out of your wallet and put them willy nilly into a clutchpurse that you know you're only going to use once or twice a month, and then not put them back, when you know they're necessary to conceive a child?! Why do you do that?!

JULIET. *(on verge of tears)* Because I'm stupid?

JIM. *(pulling driver's license out of his pocket)* Here. I saw the purse on the bureau, and I knew what you'd done. Go sign in.

JULIET. Thank you, Jim. I don't know what I'd do without him!

(JULIET *exits.*)

(uncomfortable silence)

(They sit, a few chairs between them.)

JIM. She's not usually like that.

JOAN. The whole scenario is very familiar.

JIM. She's a good person.

JOAN. And I'm not?

JIM. I didn't say that.

JOAN. You practically did. Fuck off, Jim.

JIM. So hostile.

(beat)

JOAN. And I'm not alone.

JIM. What?

JOAN. I'm not alone, like you said. "That's why you're still alone." How do you know I'm still alone? It's been thirteen months. You met someone. Why couldn't I?

JIM. I just assumed.

JOAN. Well, you're wrong.

JIM. I'm sorry.

JOAN. Yeah.

JIM. That's great news.

JOAN. Yeah. It is.

JIM. Where is he?

JOAN. Right - here.

> *(Enter* **BOB,** *with a clipboard – with a form on it – and a pen. He's puzzling over it.)*
>
> Bob! Bob, where did you run off to? We've got an egg retrieval today.

BOB. Huh?

JOAN. Come sit by me. Let me help you with that form.

BOB. They gave me a form.

JOAN. I know, let's look it over.

JIM. Wow, hey.

BOB. Hey.

JIM. You guys are both in costume.

JOAN. Yes, that's how you know we're together.

JIM. Are you going to some kind of costume party?

BOB. A party for Yahweh.

JOAN. We're going to church, Jim.

JIM. But you're Jewish. I thought you were doing a favor for a friend.

JOAN. A *boy*friend, Jim. Bob's Christian and we're playing Joseph and Mary in the Christmas story later today.

BOB. In different churches.

JOAN. We're doing a tour of churches.

BOB. I'm doing just one church.

JOAN. I'm the keeper of the schedule. He doesn't know.

JIM. Well, we're just having dinner with Juliet's rich parents.

JOAN. Well, we like to be of service, Jim.

BOB. *(referring to his clipboard)* I don't understand a lot of these questions.

JOAN. So we'll go over them.

BOB. They said I could apply to be a sperm donor.

JOAN. Well, you don't have to apply. You're *my* donor.

BOB. I am??

JOAN. Yes, Bob, that's the plan. Remember, we talked about all of this before.

BOB. I tune out a lot in conversations. I guess I missed that.

JIM. It's an easy thing to miss.

JOAN. So, let's fill this out and stay focused, okay, Bob? See, Jim, I help him focus.

JIM. Sounds like you've found the perfect match.

BOB. It asks here, have I done this before? I've done *this* lots of times before.

JOAN. You have?

BOB. Maybe a thousand times. I confess afterwards, but I still keep doing it.

JOAN. I think they just mean doing it, *in a facility like this.*

BOB. Okay, then it's my first time.

JOAN. That's what I thought.

JIM. So, Bob. You and Joan are an item, huh?

BOB. *(referring to his questionnaire)* Uh, yes. Item three, right here.

JOAN. Jim.

JIM. Ha ha. That's great. I'm really happy for you.

BOB. Thank you, Jim.

JIM. So how long have you two known each other?

BOB. Well, Jim, I'm not a real accurate measurer of time, but I'd have to say it feels to me about fifteen minutes.

JOAN. It does, doesn't it!

BOB. Yeah, it does.

JOAN. God, how time flies when you're crazy about each other.

(She puts her arm around him.)

BOB. *(pleasantly surprised.)* Okay. Next question: "Are either of your parents dwarves?" I'm going to go with "no."

JIM. That's terrific. You meet in a bar or something?

JOAN. *(with a wink at* **BOB***)* Or something!

BOB. *(plays along, not fully comprehending)* Or something!

JOAN. Some crazy place!

BOB. Some wild locale!

JOAN. Some ridiculous location!

BOB. Some insane area!

JOAN. Ha ha ha!

BOB. Ha ha ha!

BOTH BOB & JOAN. Ha ha ha!

> (JOAN *kisses* BOB *to distract everyone.*)

BOB. Wow.

> (*tiny beat*)

We met right over there.

> (JOAN *puts her head in her hands.*)

"Have you ever been bitten by an animal with rabies?" Only the twice.

JIM. You met over there, huh?

JOAN. *(as an explanation)* I've been coming here a looong time.

BOB. That's true, she has. She has the knitting to prove it.

JIM. Right.

JOAN. Jim.

JIM. What's her cat's name?

BOB. What?

JOAN. Jim.

JIM. What's her mangy old half-blind cat's name? What flavor ice cream does she eat too much of? Which musical instrument does she leave out in the living room but never actually practices to the point of any kind of mastery?

BOB. Is there an oral quiz part of this questionnaire?

JOAN. No. Jim, you don't have to be cruel. Okay, the joke's over. I'm doing it alone. I'm *alone*, okay? I don't know this guy at all. I just met him here. You win. I'm a complete and total loser.

BOB. What's happening?

JIM. You've got me all wrong, Joan. I don't want you to lose. I want to help you. All I want to do is help you achieve your potential. And you're clearly slipping.

JOAN. Yeah, whatever.

BOB. Wait, does this mean I'm not going to be your donor?

JOAN. No, Bob. I'm sorry. I'm not feeling very well. I'm sorry. I have to go.

(**JOAN** *starts to pack her knitting in her bag in a flustered hurry.*)

JIM. *(stops her on her way out)* Wait, Joan. Listen, I feel bad about – everything. And, since you have no one and clearly, the quality of anonymous sperm donors in this places is iffy…While I'm in the booth in there, making the magic for my beautiful wife – If you want to me to fill another specimen cup for you, I will. Free of charge. Long as we keep it on the downlow from the missus, and you don't come after me for college tuition.

JOAN. Goodbye, Jim.

JIM. You sure?

JOAN. Please get out of my way.

JIM. A little splurt of Jimmy for old times' sake? It's the best you'll do.

JOAN. Enough! Okay? Enough! There's nothing wrong with me. There is nothing wrong with me!

JIM. Then why are you all alone?

(*beat*)

BOB. She's not alone.

JIM. What?

BOB. You said, why are you all alone. She's not alone!

JIM. Bob, I know this is above your chromosomal level, but I'm not talking about friends. I'm talking about the father.

BOB. She's not alone because she's having God's baby! She's too special to have your baby! She's having God's! And I'm going to help take care of them! Because I'm Joseph!

JIM. I thought you were Bob.

BOB. *(stands)* Whatever. Same difference.

JIM. *(real alpha-male, gives* **BOB** *a push)* Yeah, you know what, retard?

BOB. *(immediately puts* **JIM** *into a painful head lock)* What, asshole?

JIM. Aaagghh.

   (Enter **JULIET.***)*

JULIET. Jim? Jim, stop playing. It's time.

   *(***BOB** *releases* **JIM.***)*

JIM. *(recovering)* You – You – You're lucky I have to go in there and jerk off!

   *(***BOB** *faces him down.* **JIM** *slinks off with* **JULIET.***)*

   C'mon, let's go.

JULIET. I just hope your sample is good enough this time.

JIM. I've been wearing the refrigerated underpants.

JULIET. Okay, well, I hope…

   (They exit.)

   (beat)

   *(***JOAN** *sits down.* **BOB** *sits next to her.)*

JOAN. Thank you.

BOB. You're going to make a miracle, Joan. I know it.

   (She smiles at him.)

JOAN. *(shyly)* I – think you're right.

   (Lights narrow onto her in a spotlight.)

   (She touches her belly. Something has changed. She looks up.)

   (blackout)

End of Play

TWO LAST NOTES:

1) Topical references in comedy tend to age quickly, so here are a few thoughts to keep your production of *CHRISTMAS SHORTS* fresh:

GOING HOME

Jessica Simpson can be replaced by any female pop singer of the moment who is obviously not Jewish (the more vapid, the better.)

Metallica will last forever. But just in case they don't, any well-known heavy metal band should fit the bill. I suspect that Ol' Dirty Bastard and Yo Yo Ma will also persevere, but if not, I'd suggest going with the edgiest rapper and the purist classical musical luminary your audience will recognize.

Changing the artists' names should not change the lyrics of the songs Greg sings.

THE CHRISTMAS WITCH

The Ultimate Fighter (should its glorious run ever come to an end) can be replaced by any super-macho reality TV series that has been on the air for a few seasons. If you can't think of any, please use the apt (but fictional) "America's Greatest Car Crashes, Season 3...etc."

Whatever the show title, the season #'s should remain the same.

2) If you worry that the Ol' Dirty Bastard-ized lyrics that end *GOING HOME* will prove too much for your audience, I offer this PG version as a replacement:

VOICE OF OL' DIRTY BASTARD (V.O.)
'Twas the Night Before Christmas
And all through the yard
Not a creature was stirring
'Cept this *one prison guard...*"

ABOUT THE PLAYWRIGHT

MATT HOVERMAN's plays include *In Transit* (2006 FringeNYC Best Playwriting Award), *The Student* (2009 Samuel French OOB Short Play Festival Winner, 2010 Actors Theatre of Louisville Heideman Award finalist), *The Audience* (co-book writer, three 2005 Drama Desk Award nominations, including Best New Musical), *The Collectors, Beddy-Bye & High School Reunion* (2006, 2007 & 2008 Heideman Award finalists), *Searching For God In Suburbia* (2007 Huntington Theatre's Breaking Ground New Play Festival & semi-finalist, 2008 O'Neill Festival), *Christmas Shorts* (2008 Naked Angels "Angels in Progress" Workshop), *Who You See Here* (2009 Barrow Group Production & currently optioned by legendary Broadway producer Nelle Nugent) and many others.

He has been produced or developed by Naked Angels, the Transport Group, the Barrow Group, the Huntington, the Soho Playhouse, the Lark, the Axial Theatre Co., the Miranda Theatre Co., the Vital Theatre Co., the Algonquin Theatre, Blessed Unrest and more. He was a 2008 Edward Albee Foundation Fellow and the winner of two 2008 Edelman Studios "Pitch Club" Awards.

As an actor: Yale Rep, The Acting Company, La Jolla Playhouse (with directors Joseph Chaikin, John Rando, Marion McClinton, Mike Alfreds), Late Night w/Conan O'Brien and many voices for the cartoons *Pokemon, Yu-Gi-Oh!, Sonic X, WinX Club, Chaotic, Teenage Mutant Ninja Turtles.*

As a teacher and director, he has midwived the creation of over 150 solo shows, including 2010 FringeNYC Best Solo Show Award winner *Scared Skinny* (Mary Dimino), 2009 FringeNYC Best Solo Show Award Winner *Truth Values* (Gioia De Cari), 2008 FringeNYC Best Actress Award winner *Hot Cripple* (Hogan Gorman), 2008 MITF Best Solo Show Award winner *Sacred is the New Profane* (Cheryl Harnest) and 2005 FringeNYC Best Solo Show Award winner *Bridezilla Strikes Back!* (Cynthia Silver).

Brown University, B.A. in Playwriting (where he was admitted into Paula Vogel's graduate playwriting workshop as an undergrad and won the Thomas Carpenter Theatre Award); University of California, San Diego; MFA in Acting.